Copyright © 2005 by the Richard Scarry Corporation. All rights reserved under
International and Pan-American Copyright Conventions. Published in the United States
by Random House Children's Books, a division of Random House, Inc., New York, and
simultaneously in Canada by Random House of Canada Limited, Toronto.

www.randomhouse.com/kids

Library of Congress Cataloging-in-Publication Data
Gerver, Jane E.
Richard Scarry's Chuckle with Huckle! / by Jane E. Gerver.
   p. cm.
"A Bright and Early Book."
SUMMARY: Simple rhyming text presents the various activities of the animals of
Busytown.
ISBN 0-375-83166-5 (trade) — ISBN 0-375-93166-X (lib. bdg.)
[1. Animals—Fiction. 2. City and town life—Fiction. 3. Stories in rhyme.] I. Title:
Chuckle with Huckle! II. Scarry, Richard. III. Title.
PZ8.3.G3275Ri 2005
[E]—dc22 2004011361

Printed in the United States of America First Edition 10 9 8 7 6 5 4 3 2

BRIGHT AND EARLY BOOKS and colophon and RANDOM HOUSE and colophon are registered
trademarks of Random House, Inc.

Richard Scarry's

CHUCKLE WITH HUCKLE!

And Other Funny Easy-to-Read Stories

Written by Jane E. Gerver

A Bright and Early Book

From BEGINNER BOOKS
A Division of Random House, Inc.

CHUCKLE, HUCKLE!

Huckle pulls on pants.
One leg, two legs.

Too small! Not right!
Chuckle, Huckle!

Huckle pulls on pants.
One leg, two legs.

Too big! Not right!
Chuckle, Huckle!

Huckle puts on a belt.
Buckle, Huckle.

Too tight!
Not right!

Buckle,
Huckle!

Too loose! Not right!
Chuckle, Huckle!

Not loose. Not tight.
Just right!

WAKE AND BAKE

Time to wake!
Time to bake!

Take this.
Take that.

Bake this.
Bake that.

Shake up!
Wake up!

Splat!
This cake is flat!

Splat! Splat! Splat!
Flat! Flat! Flat!

Take this cake.

And this cake,

and this cake,

and that
cake.

What a cake!
Yum.

POP, TOP, POP!

Cop on the street.

Meet and greet.

Cop stops.
Top pops!

Whoosh!

Hop. Hop. Hop.
Flop! Flop! Flop!

Cop stops.
Cop on top.

Cop mops.

Cop on street.
Meet and greet.
How sweet!